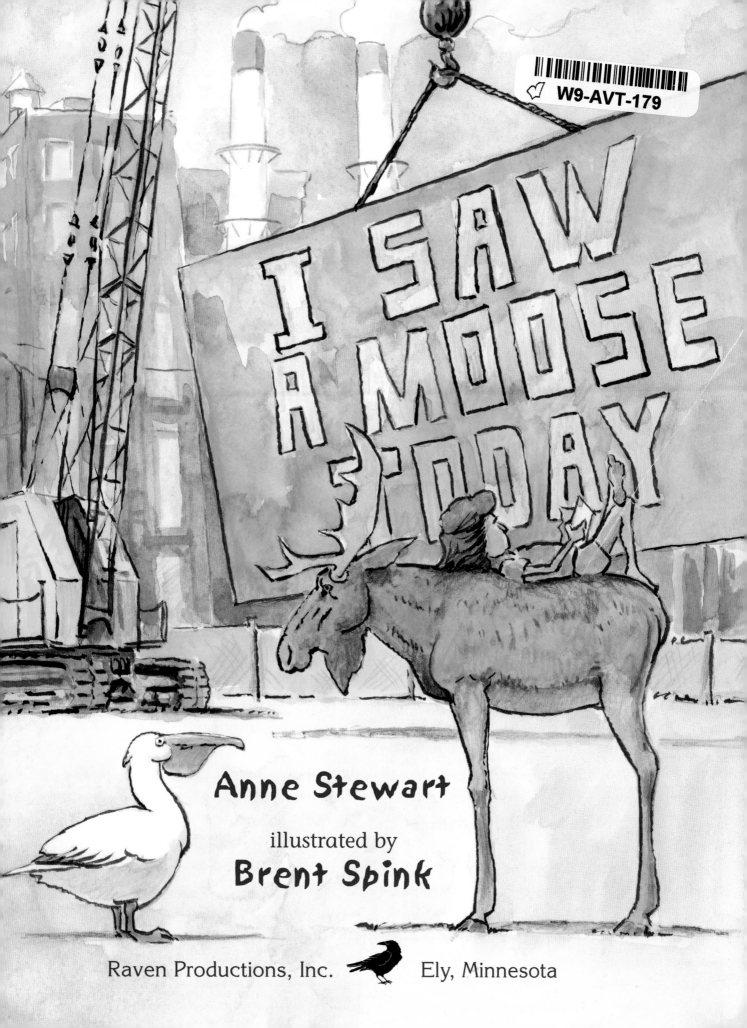

I SAW A MOOSE TODAY

Anne Stewart

illustrated by
Brent Spink

Raven Productions, Inc.　　Ely, Minnesota

For Emily Sinclair Bevis
Taylor Stewart Uehling
Matthew Thomas Uehling
Anna Caroline Uehling and Paige Victoria Uehling

In memory of
Sandra Sinclair Goulding Stuart and Gertrude Guard Bevis

– A.S.

For my family

– B.S.

Text © 2006 by Anne Stewart
Illustrations © 2006 Brent Spink

Published 2007 by Raven Productions, Inc.
PO Box 188, Ely, MN 55731
218-365-3375 www.ravenwords.com

Printed in Minnesota
United States of America
10 9 8 7 6 5 4 3 2 1

Library of Congress Cataloging-in-Publication Data

Stewart, Anne, 1936-
 I saw a moose today / Anne Stewart ; illustrated by
Brent Spink.
     p. cm.
 ISBN-13: 978-0-9766264-6-6 (hardcover : alk.
paper)
 ISBN-13: 978-0-9766264-7-3 (pbk. : alk. paper)
 1. Moose--Juvenile literature. I. Spink, Brent, 1958-
ill. II. Title.
 QL737.U55S757 2007
 599.65'7--dc22
                                        2006031742

My folks said "Today
we're cleaning the house. Please go out and play,
but *stay in the yard,* Whims Wiggin. *Don't stray!"*

I swung in my swing, made seven sand pies,
did somersaults…

WHOA!   Here was a surprise…

I saw a MOOSE today.

In MY yard!   Thought I, "A tree's in my way."
Until I perceived the tree had a knee,
and when I looked up, way up, I could see

a great, giant head and mammoth moose rack.
I shinnied his leg right onto his back,
said "Giddy up, Moose!"
He went!
Wow, he flew,
me sitting on top!
A splendid, fine view

of oceans and mountains
far from our town.
We galloped for miles
and never slowed down.

He stopped.
Off I sailed,
a thousand miles' flight,
to land in my yard.

Well…

That's not quite right.

I might see a moose if he stood and ate
the plants in the pond that's just past our gate.

But I'm sure…

I saw a **LOON** today.

She called to me in that loony loon way.
I answered her back, my fanciest call.
She asked I attend that evening's ball.

The loons wore black ties. Four mink played bassoons.
We danced and we swam and yodeled loon tunes.
We captured, down deep, a hundred-pound fish
and baked it in sauce, an exquisite dish.

At midnight a loon called, "Friends, time to go.
Let's migrate down south before winter's snow."
I watched the loons lift from water to air...

Now wait, the fact is...

I wasn't there.

I peeked through our fence, I didn't go out.
Perhaps on the pond two loons swam about,

But I'm very sure...

I saw a BEAR today.

Just ambling along the shore of the bay.
She offered her paw,
and though we'd just met,
together we sang a bold bear duet.

We picked sweet red berries covered with dew
and then had a picnic, only we two.
I tickled her tummy,
she tickled mine.
Said I, "Let's be friends."
Bear answered,
"How fine."

Bear looked at her watch, said,
"Whoops, it's quite late.
So quick! My pajamas… I hibernate."
I tucked her in snugly,
kissed her good night.

Well, no…

That's a made up story all right.

I stayed in my yard and never beyond.
I looked for a bear
down there by the pond.

But I'm very, very sure…

I saw a **BAT** today.

I wanted to swing,
  but found in the way
this little brown bat who hung by his toes.
  I climbed on my swing.
    We stared nose to nose.

Mosquitoes swarmed by. Before I could blink
Bat flew up and snatched one quick as a wink,
  smiled, "Have a mosquito!
    Tasty, mmm… Good."
I shook my head no. "I don't think I should."

We swung in my swing, sailed off hitting square
  a big hollow tree. Bat's family lived there.
They woke from their sleep
  when day turned to night.
We flew to the moon…

All right…
              Well I might

fly high with a bat I found in my swing.
Imagine what fun to do such a thing!

But I'm
    very,
        very,
            very sure…

I saw a **BEAVER** today.

She signed with her paw for me to come play.
I ran to the pond. *Kersplash!* In I leapt,
took hold of her tail, down river we swept

past turtles and fish. Two otter called, "Ho!
We want to come, too." We all dove below.
Almost out of breath, we came up for air
inside Beaver's lodge. She served birch eclair

and showed us about. We swam back outside
and tumbled down rapids. That was a ride!
Then, splashing and laughing, waded to shore.
I said a farewell...

No...

Here's the true score:

I watched through the gate with good old dog Sam,
and hoped I'd see beavers building a dam.

But I'm very,

very,

very,

very sure...

I saw a *LUNA CATERPILLAR* today.

Light green with red bumps, he wore a beret.
Blown here by the wind, he landed *kerplop,*
    right next to my toe, said "Ouch! Where'd I stop?"

    "Right here," I replied. "Do stay until noon."
    Smiled Catt, "Let us nap. I'll weave a cocoon."
    Catt wrapped us up snug, like bugs in a rug.
        We woke, tried to move,
            breathed in, gave a tug.

        "You've grown," I said.
                Catt's cocoon was too tight.
        At last we crawled out—
            a marvelous sight:
        a feather-light moth.
            Catt flew in the sky
                on swallowtail wings.

            I wish…
                        OK. I…

    I dreamed that a wondrous
            luna did things
            like weave a cocoon,
                    grow beautiful wings…

    But I'm very, very, very sure…

I saw a LYNX today.

A stubby-tailed cat, she snoozed where she lay
  stretched out on Sam's house.
She woke, yawned and frowned,
  then growled and sprang down by me on the ground.

You bet I was scared, but asked "Tell me why
  your paws are so big." Lynx did not reply.
She grasped, with her teeth, my shirt at the back,
  jumped over our fence; I hung like a sack.

We stopped far up north in very deep snow.
  "With snowshoes for feet," said Lynx,
    "watch me go."
We made a big snowlynx,
  played and had fun—
              until past my bedtime!

  Ah...

            No lynx. None!

But if snow were falling,
  coming down hard,
I might find
  some lynx tracks
    here in my yard.

            But I'm very, very sure...

I saw a
PILEATED WOODPECKER
today.

"Your beak is so big," said I. "What's it weigh?"
He rudely ignored me. He wouldn't speak.
He pounded a tree with his long, strong beak.

A fast *rat-a-tat,* a sound like a drum.
I added my own cacophonous hum.
What music we made! A rock-and-roll sound.
The tree frogs in pairs
danced merrily round.

The party broke up at quarter-till-noon,
when Dad called,
"Whims Wiggin! Lunch will be soon."

A *ha-ha-ha-ha* and Woodpecker flew
away to the woods.

Or could it be true...
he flew in that hole
up there in the tree?

Right next to our porch—
that's where he might be.

But I'm very sure...

Dad's calling again, "For today

we're done cleaning house. Come in right away,
Whims Wiggin, for lunch."

But I want to stay
out here with old Sam.

I might see…
Oh, wow!
I'm sure that I see......

"Whims Wiggin. Right *now!*"

I'm sure I have to go in for lunch.

MOOSE

DID YOU KNOW that male moose, called bulls, have antlers that weigh as much as 75 pounds? Heavy-duty ligaments in a moose's neck connect his head to his body, and extra strong muscles make it possible for the moose to lower his head with those heavy antlers on top, take a bite of food, and then raise his head back up. In winter the antlers fall off. The shed antlers are food for mice, voles, and porcupines. A bull moose grows new antlers each summer. Native Americans used moose antlers to make glue, arrow tips, and tools.

The female moose, called cows, have one or two calves in the spring. At birth a calf weighs about 30 pounds and is quite helpless. When it is a few days old, a calf can run faster than you and is also an excellent swimmer. By October it may weigh 400 pounds.

CAN YOU FIND OUT*?* How fast can a moose run? Is a moose better at seeing, hearing, or smelling? What does a moose eat? How much does it eat in a day?

LOON

DID YOU KNOW *that* loons can easily dive deep in the water but have a hard time taking off to fly? All of a loon's bones, like yours, are filled with marrow. Most birds have some bones filled with marrow and some with air, making the birds light and able to take flight easily. Since a loon doesn't have any air-filled bones, it is heavier than most birds. To take off to fly, a loon flaps its wings and runs on top of the water for a long way. A loon can't take off from land. Once in the air, the loon can fly as fast as sixty miles an hour.

A loon's heavy body helps it sink and move underwater easily. A loon swims fast underwater because its webbed feet are far back on its body and act like propellers to help it zoom along. Diving quickly and moving fast allow a loon to chase and catch the fish it eats.

Fossils of loons have been found that are 65 million years old. **CAN YOU FIND OUT***?* What are four different calls a loon makes? Why is it dangerous for a loon to be on land? Where do loons nest? Why do loon chicks ride on their parents' backs?

BEAR

DID YOU KNOW that black bears can smell their way home? A black bear seems to construct a map in its head when it travels. Part of that map information may be smells. A bear has a hundred times more area of nose membrane than you have, and so its ability to smell is much better. Scientists who study black bears have found that a bear moved 150 miles from its home territory often finds its way back home. The scientists think perhaps the bear is guided by the mapped memory of smells along the way and by the smells from its home territory.

When a bear is ready to hibernate, it looks for a snug rock crevice, a space under a log or tree root, or another protected place. A pregnant female needs to find a larger space because her cubs will be born in January or February while she is hibernating.

CAN YOU FIND OUT? In what areas of North America do black bears live? How can a black bear sleep for many weeks and not eat or go to the bathroom? What does a black bear eat? What are some other kinds of bears? How are they different from black bears?

BAT

DID YOU KNOW that little brown bats catch their food in a basket? A bat's wings are formed by thin skin that stretches over its long finger bones and attaches along its arms and down its body to its ankles. The skin also stretches from inside each leg to its tail. The bat can make a basket by tucking its tail under its body. To catch an insect, the bat flies over it and scoops the insect into the basket. The bat then ducks its head under its body, takes the insect from the basket, and gobbles up the bug.

CAN YOU FIND OUT? What is echolocation? How many insects can a bat catch in a minute? In an hour? Where do bats hang out? Do all bats eat insects? What do bats do in winter? What is the smallest bat in the world?

BEAVER

DID YOU KNOW that beavers can close their lips in back of their teeth? A beaver needs to bite and chew underwater to build its dam and lodge and to gather and store food. The skin at the sides of the beaver's lips is like a flap. To keep water out of its mouth when it works underwater, a beaver can suck in the flap to close behind its teeth. A beaver also has a valve that closes to keep water out of its nose and other valves that keep water out of its ears. Like you, a beaver's tongue and a flap over its windpipe keep water from going down its throat, but a beaver can stay under water longer than you. A beaver can stay under water for as long as five minutes.

A beaver's webbed back feet are useful in pushing it along in the water when it is swimming and diving. In the water a beaver uses its wide tail as a rudder to steer. **CAN YOU FIND OUT?** How much can a grown beaver weigh? How many beavers usually live in a lodge? What does a beaver eat? How does a beaver use its tail? How does a beaver get in and out of its lodge? What materials does a beaver use to build its dam?

LUNA CATERPILLAR

DID YOU KNOW that when luna caterpillars are inside their cocoons, they turn into a sort of slushy? After a caterpillar spins its cocoon it is called a pupa. The pupa goes through a big change called metamorphosis. Special chemicals released by the pupa's body break down many of the cells into a creamy mixture. The cells that are left reorganize to create a moth body.

When the luna moth comes out of the cocoon, it has only a few days to live. It doesn't have a mouth because it doesn't need to eat. The female moth releases special scents called pheromones which a male moth can detect up to five miles away. When a male finds the female, they mate, she lays eggs, the eggs hatch into caterpillars, and the life cycle starts over again. **CAN YOU FIND OUT?** What does a luna caterpillar like to eat? How many body sections does a caterpillar have? How many legs does a caterpillar have? How big is a luna moth? What is the difference between a moth and a butterfly?

LYNX

DID YOU KNOW that lynxes and snowshoe hares have feet that are perfect for traveling in snow? Both have large, snowshoe-like feet that make it easier to travel on top of deep snow.

In the winter about three-fourths of a lynx's menu is snowshoe hares. A lynx can't run fast for very long, so it hides along a hare's trail and waits. When the hare hops by, the lynx bounds out and catches it, unless the hare manages to escape.

Hares have a population cycle of about ten years. The number of hares increases for several years then suddenly decreases. When the hare population drops, so does the number of lynxes. When there are too few hares, lynx kittens born in the spring often die before winter, and up to 40 percent of the lynx population may starve.

CAN YOU FIND OUT? What is unusual about a lynx's feet? What does a lynx's tail look like? Its ears? What do lynxes eat besides snowshoe hares? On a map, find the areas where lynxes live. Do lynxes live near your home? How large is a lynx's home range?

PILEATED WOODPECKER

DID YOU KNOW that pileated woodpeckers have air in their heads? As a young woodpecker grows, bones form an air chamber in its head. This may act as a cushion to protect its brain when the woodpecker pounds on trees with its beak. Also, the beak is attached to the woodpecker's skull by a special bone that acts as a shock absorber.

A pileated woodpecker bores holes in trees to make a nest and to find insects for food. To capture its food, a woodpecker reaches into the hole with its long, sticky, barbed tongue.

If you see a pileated woodpecker's nest hole, scratch the bottom of the tree with a small stick. The woodpecker may look out to see who is there.

CAN YOU FIND OUT? How big is a pileated woodpecker? Which insect is the woodpecker's favorite food? How does a woodpecker know if there are insects in a tree? How does a woodpecker signal its territory to other birds?

FIND OUT MORE!

Look in your library, search the web, and visit museums, zoos, environmental learning centers and nature centers.

WEBSITES WITH MANY ANIMALS

www.kidsplanet.org
Click on "Get the Facts," then choose the animal you want to study.

www.hww.ca
Go to "Species" in the menu, then click on "Boreal Forest Species Fact Sheets." Choose your animal.

www.wikipedia.org
Choose your language, then type the name of the animal you want to find in the "Search" box. Use an underscore for animals with two words in their names, like this: luna_moth.

www.nhptv.org/natureworks
Click on "Nature Files" and choose the animal or subject that interests you.

WEBSITES FOR SPECIFIC ANIMALS

www.bear.org
Click on "Kids' Area" for black bear pictures and facts.

www.birds.cornell.edu/allaboutbirds/birdguide
Select the bird you want to study from the alphabetical list.

www.journeynorth.org
Click on "Archives," then click on "Search" and type in "loon."

BOOKS

Here are just a few of the many books about the animals in Whims's imagination:

Moose by Anthony D. Fredericks
Loons: Diving Birds of the North by Donna Love
Black Bears by Kathy Feeney and John F. McGee
When I Lived with Bats by Faith McNulty
Beavers by Deborah Hodge
Caterpillars by Barrie Watts
Lynxes by Barbara Keevil Parker and Duane F. Parker
Woodpeckers by Cherie Winner

WHIMS'S BIG WORDS

Ambling	**am** bling	Moving slowly and easily along
Bassoons	ba **soons**	Woodwind instruments with a low voice
Beret	b **ray**	A round, flat cap for the head
Cacophonous	ka **koff** uh nus	Sounding out of tune and noisy
Cocoon	kuh **koon**	A silky cover that caterpillars make by wrapping thread, and sometimes leaves, around themselves
Duet	doo **et**	Two making music together
Eclair	ay **clair**	A cream-filled pastry with icing on the outside
Exquisite	**ek** skwiz it	Very fine and well made
Hibernate	**hi** ber nate	Sleep for many months in the winter without waking up to eat, drink, or go to the bathroom
Ignored	ig **nord**	Did not pay attention to
Imagine	ih **maj** in	Picture things in the mind
Mammoth	**mam** oth	Very, very large
Marvelous	**mar** veh lus	Causes wonder
Migrate	**my** grate	To leave one place and move to another
Mosquitoes	mu **skee** toes	Flying, pesky insects that bite and suck blood
Perceived	per **seevd**	Noticed something by seeing, hearing, smelling, or feeling it
Pileated	**pie** lee ay tid	Having a feathery top or crest on the head
Shinnied	**shin** eed	Climbed up using arms and knees
Snoozed	**snoozd**	Took a short nap
Splendid	**splen** did	Grand
Stubby	**stub** ee	Short, cut off
Swarmed	**swarmd**	Flew or moved together in a group
Wondrous	**won** drus	Awesome
Yodeled	**yoh** duld	Made a musical sound in the throat; something like a musical gargle

For a language arts activity guide, check our website at www.ravenwords.com

ANNE STEWART, a writer and editor, lives in the woods north of Ely, Minnesota, where she is regularly entertained by the wild critters that pass by her house.

She writes mostly for newspapers and periodicals, but has published in an eclectic range of genre that includes history texts for middle school children, business manuals, and poetry.

Her work experience includes directing conferences and women's programs, waitressing, and teaching.

BRENT SPINK, an artist, was born in Minneapolis in 1958. He has lived and travelled in many parts of the country. The Northwoods is where he derives inspiration for his artwork and his life.

Brent has expressed his artistic talent primarily through painting, but recently he has applied his interest in form and color to working with stained glass and glass blowing. Brent divides his time between his home near Kalamazoo, Michigan, and his cabin in northern Minnesota.

RAVEN PRODUCTIONS, INC. is an independent publisher located in Ely, Minnesota. Its mission is to encourage children and grown-ups to explore, enjoy, and protect the natural world and share experiences with one another through story-telling, writing, and art. Awards for Raven Productions' books include the John Burroughs List of Nature Books for Young Readers, the Sigurd Olson Nature Writing Award for Children's Literature, and Midwest Book Awards Honorable Mention for History. You can find out more at www.ravenwords.com.